The Knitting Chicken
Copyright © 2018, 2016 Travis M. Blair
Text: Travis M. Blair
Illustration: David Buist

Second Edition
Editor: Amy Waeschle

ISBN: 978-0-692-08076-4

Published by Zarfling Platoon
info@zarfling.com
zarfling.com

FROM THE
HEARTY
EGGS
FARM
COLLECTION

For Emi, Sofia, Xander, and Skylar
–T.B.

For Tracy, Lily, Sophie, and Claire
– D.B.

On a warm summer day at Hearty Eggs Farm,
fifty chatting chickens are hard at work.
They work for Farmer Hank, a kind and fair boss.

These chickens' only job is to lay eggs, and many of them. The farm is also home to cows for milk and sheep for wool, but the farm is best known for its eggs.

Every morning, Farmer Hank collects the eggs from all of the chickens in the coop. He notices one chicken has not laid any eggs since she came to the farm.

That chicken's name is Lucy.
She feels bad about not being able to lay any eggs,
and has been worried about her job. Lucy sits quietly, constantly knitting.
Her concern is apparent by the large rug she knitted for the chicken coop floor.

Lucy is so worried about her afternoon meeting
that she frantically knits a scarf for Farmer Hank.
She does not want to leave the farm,
and hopes the gift will keep her from losing her job.

Lucy has her meeting with Farmer Hank.
She is told she has three months to lay an egg.

That evening, Lucy is so sad that she paces back and forth across her knitted rug.

"What am I to do?
I don't want to go,
but I cannot lay any eggs."
Lucy asks the crowd of chickens
around her for advice.

One of the chickens tells her,

"If you don't stay at the farm, you could always go into the knitting business. With it getting so chilly lately, I wish I had a blanket just like the rug you made!"

Just then, Lucy has an idea.

Autumn has begun, and the days and nights are getting colder.
Winter is coming and is the worst time of year for laying eggs.
Lucy has three months, so she must work quickly.

Early in the morning until late in the night,
Lucy knits in preparation for winter.

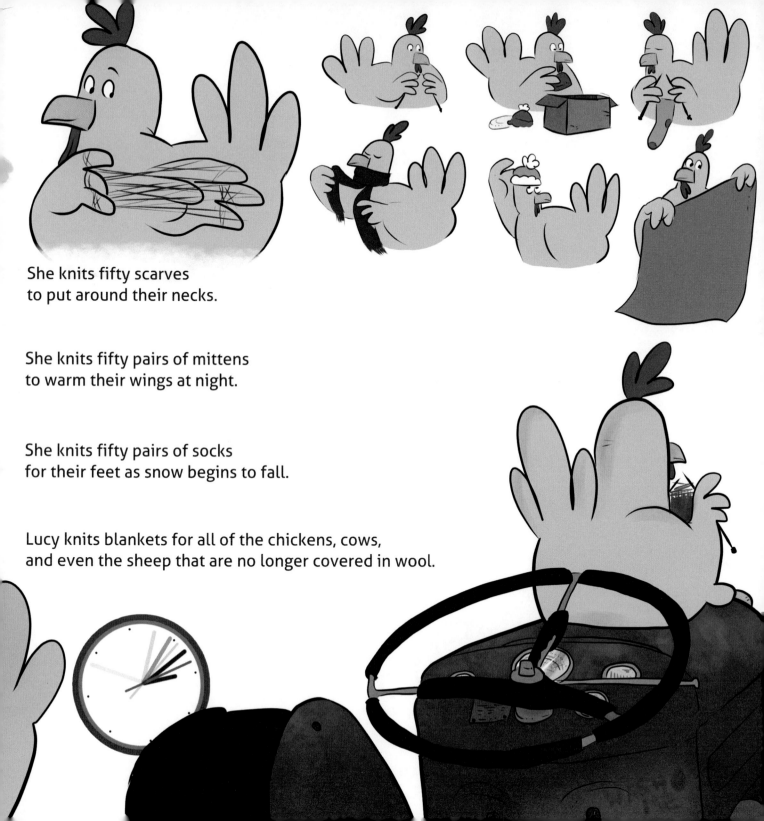

She knits fifty scarves
to put around their necks.

She knits fifty pairs of mittens
to warm their wings at night.

She knits fifty pairs of socks
for their feet as snow begins to fall.

Lucy knits blankets for all of the chickens, cows,
and even the sheep that are no longer covered in wool.

Lucy puts down her knitting needles and runs out of the coop to see her boss.
She knows three months have passed.

Farmer Hank looks over his desk at Lucy.
She looks so nervous.

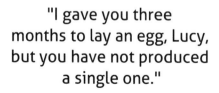

"I gave you three
months to lay an egg, Lucy,
but you have not produced
a single one."

Lucy gulps.

Farmer Hank shows Lucy a chart.
"However, this winter the chickens have stayed warm,
and we have sold the most eggs ever.
This is because of you, Lucy.
Your job at the farm is safe. I need you here."

Lucy jumps off the chair and runs around the room!
She is so happy!

On a cold winter day at Hearty Eggs Farm,
forty-nine chatting chickens keep warm in their mittens, hats, and scarves.
Cows and sheep stay warm wrapped in their blankets.

While the fiftieth chicken, Lucy, takes a well-deserved nap.

The end?

Made in the USA
Middletown, DE
04 June 2019